# The Universe Sucks: Existence is Futile

Elona Schitter

*Reluctantly* Edited by

Marq Truong

LeeLoo Publishing™ / Texas

Against better judgment, Published by
LeeLoo Publishing™
LeeLooPub.com
All rights reserved.

First Edition/Print
ISBN: 0998884324
ISBN-13:
978-0998884325

# ADVERSE REACTIONS WARNING:

Reading this book of poetry could result in some rare, but serious reactions including but not limited to: brain injury, coma, nose bleeds, ear bleeds, stroke, toe fungus, difficulty swallowing, rash, hives, blindness, cotton mouth, difficulty urinating, depression, suicidal ideation, psychotic episodes, cold sweats, anal leakage, spontaneous combustion, loss of hearing and/or death. If any of these symptoms occur, seek professional help immediately and, for crying out loud, stop reading the damned book. The less hazardous and most common side effect is a complete apathetic disdain for what poses as intelligent life in the Ultimate Universe.

ELONA SCHITTER

# DISCLAIMER AND RELEASE OF RESPONSIBILITY AND LIABILITY

LeeLoo Publishing, any of its employees and the fictional editor and author Marq Truong are in no way responsible and cannot be held liable for any injury, real or imagined, or resultant mental illness, again real or imagined, which may or may not be the product of reading this book. By purchasing or continuing to read further you waive the right to hold anyone but yourself responsible for any adverse reactions to the content of these pages (digital or otherwise).

Under the Ultimate Galactic Universe Freedom of Poetry Act, Poets are entitled and encouraged to promote the dying literary art of poetry, and thus, entitled to write poetry in any form, whatsoever, they believe to be artistic, no matter how horrendous, awful, brain damagingly terrible it is, without fear of reprisal or legal action. It is a tenth degree felony, subject to a tenth degree death penalty, to murder a poet, even in self defense, if that said self defense was to stop the assault of the poetry. The only restriction to the poet is that the poetry must represent some semblance of truth, but by the definitions of Theoretical Beology, anything that can be, is, so thus, anything postulated as true, must be true, including the truth that it is all a lie.*

*A required statement by Theoretical Intergalactic Universal Law

ELONA SCHITTER

# DEDICATION

I would dedicate this to my fans, but I don't have any. And I don't want any. And if you are reading this, your life probably sucks worse than mine.

ELONA SCHITTER

# CONTENTS

# ACKNOWLEDGMENTS

LeeLoo Publishing would like to acknowledge the fine and valiant efforts of Marq Truong for editing this work of Ultimate Galactic Literature and express our humble apologies for the months of treatment (at our expense) required to recover from the venture. The author was unavailable for comment regarding positive acknowledgments., rather, she actually said, "I'd like to acknowledge that I hate everyone." We would also like to acknowledge this is all fiction, including, but not limited to, the acknowledgment.

# CHAPTER ONE
# POETRY ABOUT STARS

## 1.0 Hot

Stars are hot.
Very hot.
They blast with unforgiving heat
and incinerate the bodies of flesh
which dare to dive too close.
Except for Salamandoreans.
They are rumored to live inside suns, but no one
knows.
Is incineration a good way to die?
Everything dies.
Almost everything.
Everything that doesn't die
is trapped in this miserable existence for eternity.
I'd rather fly into the sun
and dance with a Salamandorean.
Then die.
But I won't get to
because the stupid sun will
incinerate me
first.

## 1.1 Light

The infinite stars and star systems
cannot light all of space
which, too, is infinite.
Which doesn't make sense.
If there is infinite space and infinite light
then how can there be darkness?
But the darkness is infinite, too.
Or we don't know the difference between the light and
the dark
and it is really just
space.
The darkness is within us
the light is what we wish we could touch.
And the space goes on forever.
... the light always just out of our reach.

## 1.2 Were they?

They were bright and beautiful
gleaming rays of hope in the night sky
that promised a child
adventure
with visions of exploration and excitement.
Or were they conniving demons at play
soliciting the souls of the innocent
with lies of what the universes hold?
The stars claimed to be your friend,
but,
were they?

## 1.3 Ugh

Not UGH, Ugh.
I hate stars.
Pretending to be all glittery.
From a distance they dazzle
but the closer you get
the hotter and sweatier
you become
until you stink.
Then they cook
your flesh
and devour you,
reducing your corpse
to its most base component.
Then solar winds whisk
you away,
fodder to eternity's
endless course of destruction.

## 1.4 Vespers

kissed by the first
vespers
of the night sky
on a distant world
only few have touched
and sinking in solemn loneliness
as it is only the
light of
that distant sun
which found you
and saw the darkness inside.
But its simple, flickering light
was not enough
to fill
the void
that childish hope
had abandoned.

## 1.5 They are Idiots

"Look to the stars," they said.
Idiots.
"Let the stars be your guide," they said.
Idiots.
"Shoot for the stars," they said.
Idiots.
"Reach for the stars," they said.
Idiots.
Do they even know that stars
are giant balls of unstable gases
burning at billions of degrees?
Idiots.

## 1.6 Motion Sickness

Everything moves
The stars are not fixed into place
but fluid
and spinning
a death spiral
simultaneously
flinging all of
the universe away
and sucking it in.
We cannot escape
the push and pull
of the universal dance.
Come here
Go there
Be this
Do that
we are spinning
in circles of confusion
unable to grasp the beat of the music
or find rhythm
to steady ourselves.
Unable to feel reason.
We spin until
the illness of it consumes us.

## 1.7 Happy Sunshine

Yeah. You wish.
The sun is not happy.
None of them are happy.
They don't make you happy.
They do not feel or express feelings.
They do not react to your emotions.
For all the heat they thrash into the universes
their hearts are cold.

## 1.8 Sun of a Bitch

Because there actually is
a sun
that belongs
to a female
dog.
My father
bought his dog,
Lulu,
a small,
blue sun
in Quadrant IV.
Which makes it
the
Sun of a Bitch.
I found it
poetic.
But I still
hate
that
spoiled
dog.

## 1.9 No Stars

were there no stars
there would be no light
there would be no planets teeming with life
no ships zipping about space
no fashionable donut planet
no frat boys interrupting
when someone they assume is female
speaks
no infinite corporate battles
over the flavors of soda
and no mind numbing professors
indoctrinating young minds
to think as they are told to think
-which is to not think at all.
There would be darkness.
And in that darkness
a profound silence
and peace.
Suns.
We could do without them.
It would save everyone time.
It is easier
not to think for yourself
when you don't exist

# CHAPTER TWO
# POETRY ABOUT DOORS

## 2.0. Doorknob

I saw a doorknob,
ancient
in a museum
and its function was to open a door.
Beings grasped it, firmly
and twisted
and a mechanism unlatched the door
so that it could be pushed open.
So much work.
So much effort.
We evolved to build
doors which open themselves
doors that even guess where you would like to go
But did we ever think
If we didn't build walls
we wouldn't need doors at all?

## 2.1 Lift

I stared out the lift doors
down a hallway of domiciles,
flickering lights,
and a dank,
sad
smell
of decay and neglect.
Should I hit a different floor?
Make another button happy?
Would it be any different?
Or do all lift doors
lead to
awaiting misery?

## 2.2 Doorways

How many do we walk through
each day?
How many of the same doorways?
How many times do we enter the same room,
the same home,
the same business?
What draws us back
over and over
to what we already know?
What drives us away,
out the door
and into the
empty other
awaiting
beyond?
Why are we
forever
conflicted
between the security
we crave
and the
freedom
we relish?

## 2.3 Closed Doors

I was told in
my disappointment
that when one door closes
another opens.
But that is stupid.
They say you can't go back
once that door is closed.
But why not?
Isn't that
how doors
work?
Isn't that what they do?
They open.
They close.
They open again.
They close again.
Better to ask, maybe
with all the doors in the universe
why would you want to keep traversing
the same threshold
over and over?
Given the choice,
would you really go back?
What is behind that door
which you cannot find
anywhere else?
And if it was so important
what are you doing on this side of it?
Life sucks glebular succor worm butts.

If it is going to close the door, anyway,
beat it all
by slamming it first.

## 2.4 Archways

I hate archways
decorative pieces of
preppy yard
dung.
What are they?
Are they doors from nowhere to nowhere?
Hello?
What is this stupid shit?
I like arches covered in
carnivorous roses.
Those are funny.

## 2.5  Do not enter

I closed the door
I locked the door
I put up a sign
"Do not Disturb"
and another
"Go away."
and I tried to sleep.
But things kept creeping through
along the edges
under the door
seeping into my solitude
refusing to leave me alone.
No matter how hard I try
to close myself away
to hide
I cannot
escape
myself.

## 2.6. Exit Only

I saw an exit only sign
and wondered why.
What would happen if I did not exit?
And then I thought, aren't all doors
exits only?
Aren't you always leaving
where you are?
Aren't all doors
entrances
to where you are going?
Are Entrance and Exit
really just two words
for the same action?

## 2.7 No Door Out

In this infinite
universe of
infinite universes,
gamboling from one to the next,
there is no
door out
and no door in
only shifting
nuances from one room of infinity
to
the next.
We travel in circles
of
nowhere
searching for
nothing.

## 2.8 Photons

Sentients think themselves
so clever
dividing up
miniscule segments
of infinity-
chopping it to pieces,
boxing it up
with walls
and borders-
doors leading in
and out-
and selling it off
to one another
as though it were a
finite resource.
But no one can own infinity.
It laughs at our
infantile
gestures
to constrain it.
It will exist
even after
all the suns have gone super nova
and nothing remains
but individual photons
floating in nothing.

## 2.9 Wormholes

Even the universe made doorways
instant portals to cover
vast distances
sometimes there
and sometimes not
some by strict schedule
and some wayward
and mischievous
ready to pop into
existence
and cart you off
to the unknown
at any time.
What if the Universe
itself
is sentient?
What if it is alive
and we
are all
simply small pieces of it?
What if the universe is
some sadistic
asshole
who thinks it is funny
to drop wormholes on
beings
and get them freaking lost
in the middle of
nowhere?

Actually,
that makes a lot of sense.
That would explain a lot.

# CHAPTER THREE
# POETRY ABOUT COLOURS

## 3.0 Orange

The vibrant child of
Yellow and (Colour Redacted)
you make me
feel warm
and hungry
and powerful
and mad.
I see you flickering in the flames of candles
and on t shirts
and velour jogging suits,
but do I know you?
Do you know me?
Are you real?
Or are you an illusion?
A dream conjured
from my grey scale
mind?

### 3.1 Green

I walked in green grass
outside a coffee shop
in Quadrant XXIX.
It felt prickly
beneath my bare feet.
It had been recently cut.
The blades sheered off
for the crime
of growing
of reaching too high.
Each bright blade was edged with sorrow
yet it
did not give up.
It refused to stop growing
it refused to stop reaching
even knowing it would be slashed and cut
viciously
again
and again.
One might look at this
and find hope;
defiant pleasure
at its refusal to die.
But I see
the dismal reality
of civilization,
where we all keep reaching and trying
to grow
to fulfill some greater purpose

to reach our full potential
only to be cut down again
and again,
for the pleasure
and purpose
of others.
We are mown
grass,
kept because we are green
and useful
kept because we keep trying.
But when we fail to be green,
we will be stripped away and replaced.
We are just here to decorate someone's lawn.

### 3.2 Red

*This poem has been censored and removed by court order because Brick Wilson purchased a copy of this book of poetry, which by definition, means he has a pretty shitty existence. The colour red is under strict court order, by way of restraining order, to not be within any reasonable distance of Mr. Wilson. The Publisher is further interpreting that, at this time, to include such descriptive references to Red as might exist in poetry, nonfiction or fictional publications, as it may conjure the image of Red in the readers' mind, making them in violation of the court order and subject to having their minds taken and locked away until such time as a hearing can be held to determine if their mind was, in fact, red, or not. We apologize for any inconvenience this may cause.

### 3.3 Yellow

I hate yellow.
It is bright
and cheerful
and too many sorority girls
wear yellow bikinis.
Yellow flowers make me sneeze.
It is a lie.
It invites you to be happy,
cajoling you
to let your guard
down
be free
inviting
innocent.
But it always abandons you.
It is the colour of childhood.
The colour of lies.
Life is not yellow.

### 3.4 Violet

The eternity of the universe
is not black.
It is a deep tinge of violet
sweeping across galaxies.
Lilting and solemnly inviting...
a sweet sadness,
because it is you
and me,
and in it,
we exist
without mortality
as nothing more
than wisps of
distant violet,
tiny fragments
of
nothing
and
everything.

### 3.5 Brown

The colour of some dirt is brown.
The most intelligent dirt, encrusting Dep Vida
-a small, sentient planet in Quadrant II-
is a deep, rich brown.
Is it the colour of intelligence?
Is it the ultimate colour of life?
Are any of us brown?
Inside?
Are we truly sentient?
Do we exist to be brown
or does brown exist within us?

### 3.6 Blue

The colour
of serenity...
the washing shades of waters, skies and beaches
of lounge chairs
and carpets
of velour jumpsuits
and sporty space vets
of wampulus trees
and suburban fences
of chipped nail polish
peeling from the tusks of
old, pompous men
whose glory days have long passed
and now
they just sit n their blue lounge chair, beneath the blue
sky
looking out over an ocean of faded memories
wearing that hideous jumpsuit
like a badge of honour
stretched too tightly across their expanding bellies.
Blue should be the colour of champions
of beauty and achievement, but
it is the colour of
want-
of what was
and is
lost-
of what even an old blue couch cannot reclaim.
It is the resentment

of youth,
the bitterness of age
and the
realization of
mortality.
Blue sucks.
If you're old.

### 3.7  Pink

I would rather like pink
if it were not just a watered down version of (colour
redacted).
But perhaps I am just a watered down version of
myself
and who I could be
if I had the compulsion
to achieve
anything.
But why?
What is there to do that hasn't been done?
Or that someone won't see you do, then
just take a couch back
and do it first?
Pink is the me that exists
in this watered down
version
of reality.

### 3.8 Grey

An ode to grey
and the disparity
of it.
The clinging edge of nothing and everything.
Grey floats along the precipice
of now
and anywhere
and anywhen
else.
Grey is the border
the no zone
the nothing
and everything
between what is
what was
what will be
and what could be.
The despair of grey
is hope.

### 3.9  Clear

Just because you cannot see it
does not mean it is not there.
The window exists
even though you can see through it.
clear is the color of
nothing
and everything
it is all that goes unseen
it is all the faces we pass
the lives we ignore
the worlds left to perish
the voices unheard
the songs unsung
to all but the dark abyss of
time
clear is what goes unnoticed as we
traverse
the rituals
of life.
It is the constant
which says life does not change
greed does not relinquish
its hold
to let our eyes stray for even
a moment
to see the
ugly reflection
we cast of ourselves.

# CHAPTER FOUR
# POETRY ABOUT BODY PARTS

### 4.0 Feet

Some use feet to walk about,
to strut
to move from one place
to another.
Some are fitted with toes
and some are just blunt things at the end of legs.
A great many
species
developed feet.
They are
the fifth most common
trait among humanoids-
yet for
all the walking and
moving about
what do they accomplish?
each is a marvel of unique complexity
yet as unthought of,
as uncared for
(until they hurt)
as assholes
-the sixth most common attribute of humanoids-
no one considers their life without feet until
they've been devoured by flesh eating
roses

or worse.
The simple action of
walking
across the room, to your space vehicle,
into a bar
are all lost on the
dimwitted
inhabitants
of the universe.
We
are specs of morons
floating through a
sea of stupidity.

## 4.1 Asshole

The asshole is an
amazing
bodily
apparatus.
It mirrors the self
in complexity and simplicity
and we all use our emotional sphincter
to close up
and hold in
all the dirty
rotten
filthy
thoughts
and emotions
churning inside us
until it builds so much pressure
-becomes so volatile...
until there is literally just too much shit to hold inside
even a moment longer
then it opens
and releases
all our vile contents out into the universe-
stinking everything up
and creating
a cesspool
of our own vulgarity.

### 4.2. Nose

Noses are amazing.
I wish I had one
or three
instead of the
efficient evolution
of
nors.
I think ears and noses should not
be combined
there are some smells you simply do not want to hear
and some sounds
that are best
left unsmelled.
I long for
quiet smells.
For us with norses
there is no such thing
as a
silent fart.

### 4.3 Neck

Men without necks
are creepy.
Squidulons do not have necks
but perhaps
millions
of appendages.
Could the neck be an appendage?
And the head like a foot
or hand?
Most species can live without a foot or hand.
But then, many can live without a head.
The Hall of Important Heads
shows us that a head can live without
a body.
So why do we have necks?
oh, right,
so that everyone doesn't
look so creepy.

## 4.4 Appendages

Arms, legs
armlegs
hands, feet
fingers, toes
penises
testicles
breasts
tentacles
ears, noses, norses
so many
strapped on
pieces
to create a single
being.
So much attention to detail,
care of craftsmanship,
millions of years of evolution
to design a
single being
whose ultimate purpose-
most fantastic desire-
is to
consume
as many hotdogs
in ten minutes
as
possible.

## 4.5 Mouth

We use our mouths to speak quiet words
of comfort
to scream
a diatribe of hate
to whisper encouragement
and sigh in relief.
We taste
we eat
we drink
we spit
we bite and chew
and suckle.
We breathe in and vomit out.
We smile and frown,
purse and clench and exclaim.
But what no one ever seems to do,
unless they are hiding
is shut their mouth.
The universe is filled with
mouths
in a constant state of motion,
never ceasing,
never shutting up.
The universe could do without mouths,
Most beings would starve to death
but that would solve a great many problems, too.
I hate mouths.

## 4.6  Ears

Not every species in the universe
has ears
Some are telepathic
some use antennae
some use their sense of smell
-they smell-hear
the world.
Some have norses instead,
which I think sucks.
Be glad if you have ears.
You would hate to smell
every hateful
thing
anyone has to say.
It is bad enough just hearing
the whining voices
of mundane
existence
without knowing
how awful
bad breath can really be
when combined
with the stupid
things they say.

### 4.7 Eyes

You think you see me.
You think you know me.
You think you see yourself,
as you are.
But you only see
what you want
what you wish were true.
You covet
a fabrication-
a fantasy-
an illusion conceived
within yourself
that begins with
the deceit
of your own
eyes.

## 4.8  Stomach

stomachs are smarter
than most beings.
they are probably
the smartest part
of the body.
They accept what is given
with open anticipation.
They know how to demand
attention.
They make those who mistreat them
suffer
horribly.
Smart.
wish I could throw acid
on things.
Maybe that is why we
are all so miserable.
Maybe our universe
is just a
giant stomach
and we are splashing about
in stomach acid.
That's gross.

### 4.9 Warts

I do not have warts.
I'm happy about that.
Some have warts on their faces,
hands,
feet,
knees,
even on their toes.
There is a species of sentient warts,
symbiotic parasites
that are illegal to kill
but can be imprisoned
for attaching to
an unwilling host.
But since you can't detach them,
the host goes to prison
too.
That is dumb,
or smart,
because you have to be really
really
really stupid
to let a
Procci Wart
attach itself to your head
without
knowing it.
Anyone that stupid
should be locked away
from the general public

because stupidity spreads
like the most
infectious disease.
In our universe
Stupid
is a plague.

# CHAPTER FIVE
# POETRY ABOUT EMOTIONS

## 5.0 Love

Love is the
beautiful spark
of promise
and hope
that keeps the universe
stable.
Love does not move planets or mountains or rivers
or stars or moons
It moves spirits
emotions
lives
and certain models
of space ships
which operate on
love drives.
It is said to be the one
truth
of the universe.
For real?
Seriously?
Love is the truth?
No thank you.
I'll pass.

## 5. Hate

Hate is not the opposite of love.
Space ships built on hate drives
get better mileage
and go faster.
Hate can feel good.
It seeks out its friends,
vengeance, rage
and spite
which appears to be
the bigger fabric
of the worlds
and existence.
it is dark matter
woven into emotion.
It is the space between the stars
and the fury of them.
But I'm not a fan.
It takes far too much energy to hate.
I'll take watered down disdain.
That's more my speed.

## 5.2 Sympathy

You know that feeling
in the pit of your stomach
when you see someone suffering-
that urge to help
that compelling
need to do something,
make them better,
to change them
or change their world
or change reality?
I didn't think
you did.
Sympathy
has become
a rare quality.
Near extinct.
No one cares
about you, about me
or about anything.

## 5.3  Happiness

Happiness is not
the smell
of fish sauce in
scrambled eggs.

## 5.4 Sadness

That lonely
emptiness
of knowing
everything you have ever
done
or will do
every experience
every word
emotion
friend you have made
victory won
everything
was futile
as it is washed away
in the grand sweep
of eternal waves.

## 5.5  Misery

Misery
is being forced
to share a cab
with a bubbly,
happy person,
who smiles genuinely
at everything
and has an infectious laugh
-so infectious
that before you know it
you are laughing, too.
Then their fare is up
and they leave
and you realise
you are still smiling
but the joy fades
and the smile becomes forced
as the vacuum
sets in.
You are alone in the back seat
of a dingy cab,
meter ticking.
Then the smile disappears,
replaced by sadness,
left as a reminder
that some people really are happy,
just not you.

## 5.6  Disgust

This swirl of the macabre,
destitute
existence
of sentient
bundles of matter
zipping about
bumping into one another
drinking sodas
singing songs
jogging in velour pant suits
and breeding flesh eating begonias
is
pretty
disgusting.
The sheer amount of waste
-fecal and otherwise-
exuded by these
patrons of society
makes glebular succor worms
sweet
by comparison.

## 5.7  Apathy

When all has been felt
and there is nothing left
in all of space
in all of existence
to fill the void
of the soul,
we slip into
the comfort,
the selfish indulgence,
of
apathy.

## 5.8  Bitterness

You want to know bitterness?
How about knowing
you would inherit
so much denari
you could change the universe?
Knowing you could end
famines,
homelessness,
poverty
and even put in
significant research
to cure stupid?
-But you can't
because
the government
needs these things
and writes laws to protect
starvation, instead of the hungry-
protect poverty instead of the impoverished-
protect stupid instead of those inflicted-
So they put a limit on the good you can do.
They say it is to keep the economy stable
but I think
it is for power
because hungry, sick, impoverished, stupid people
are easy to control.
And UGH
fears any wealth
greater than their own.

We should all be bitter-
like bitter seeds
in the government's stomach
until they
regurgitate
what they have stolen.

### 5.9 Remorse

No one is ever sorry.
They keep lying
stealing
cheating
pushing
shoving
stomping
screaming
hitting
wanting more
and more.
They take
and take
and take
until there is nothing left
then move on
leaving destruction
in their wake
and a trail of pain
behind them.
They grab everything they can get
and care not for what it costs.
who it hurts.
They do not care
about anything
or any one.
There is no remorse
until they die

and then
it won't matter
anyway.

## NOTE FROM THE EDITOR
## MARQ TRUONG

There were a subsequent five chapters dealing in subjects which became increasingly more morose and disturbing. At the point of finishing the fifth chapter, my eyes were literally bleeding, I'd been through several bottles of Tequila and had run completely out of limes. The following five chapters have been redacted, or more accurately, censored for the benefit of humanity and because they couldn't find anyone else willing to edit it. I highly suggest, if you enjoyed this, to seek professional, psychiatric help immediately and try to not interact with or influence anyone else as you make your way to the nearest inpatient facility. Also note that I highly objected to the publication of this work but the publisher told me to skip off, I'd been paid and signed the release so they were going to use my name anyway. So, I hope you survived unscathed. Have a drink (I had many) and with a few years of counseling, it should be all better.

## ABOUT THE AUTHOR

Elona Schitter prefers you know nothing about her, as she is a very private kind of being and thinks it is really none of anyone's business where she is from, what she likes or what inspires her.

ELONA SCHITTER

## NOTE FROM THE POET
## ELONA SCHITTER

Yeah, I don't give a shit if this is published or not. I don't write for the commercial enjoyment of idiots who probably don't even understand that we are all connected to this thing,

this huge, life-sucking black hole we call the universe and it sucks us all in and excretes us out in a squishy semblance of what we thought we were. No one gets it and it is so pathetic.

## MORE FROM THE
## ULTIMATE GALACTIC UNIVERSE

Brick Wilson: For Hire

Brick Wilson: Clueless

Immerse yourself in the Ultimate Galactic Universe, find events, giveaways, merchandise, contests, and email your favorite characters by visiting:

BrickWilson.com

UltimateGalacticUniverse.com

# MORE FROM
# LEELOO PUBLISHING

### Brick Wilson: For Hire
by Marq Truong

### Brick Wilson: Clueless
by Marq Truong

### Edge of Ridiculous
by Anne Coffer

### Dragon Bloode: Covet
by Mishka Williams

### Letters: Evelyn Rose Whitten
by Ann Lavendar

### Letters: Margaret Florence Baine
by Ann Lavendar

### Samiyah
by J. R. Hicks

Find these great titles and more at:
**LeeLooPub.com**

# *CHEERS!*